King Kenrick's Splinter

Sally Derby

Illustrations by Leonid Gore

Walker and Company

NEW YORK

First published in the United States of America in 1994 by Walker
Publishing Company, Inc.
Published simultaneously in Canada by
Thomas Allen & Son Canada, Limited, Markham, Ontario

Library of Congress Cataloging-in-Publication Data
Derby, Sally.
King Kenrick's splinter / Sally Derby : illustrations by Leonid Gore.
p. cm.
Summary: King Kenrick tries to ignore the painful splinter in his toe,
but he finally agrees to have it tended to so he can lead the
Hero's Day Parade.
ISBN 0-8027-8322-8 (cloth). —ISBN 0-8027-8323-6 (reinforced)
[1. Wounds and injuries—Fiction. 2. Kings, queens, rulers,
etc.—Fiction. 3. Fear—Fiction.] I. Gore, Leonid, ill. II. Title.
PZ7.D4416Ki 1994
[E]—dc20 94-4360
CIP
AC

Printed in Hong Kong

2 4 6 8 10 9 7 5 3 1

To Karl, who removes the splinters and chases the shadows —SD

To my kind, wonderful parents —LG

King Kenrick pushed back the covers and jumped out of bed. Then . . . "Ow!"

He sat back down on the bed. There under the pink skin of his big toe, he saw something long and black.

"I knew it!" he said. "I have a splinter!"

King Kenrick tried hard not to cry. He hated having splinters. Whenever he had one, the queen wanted to take it out with a needle and tweezers.

"Oh dear. Today is the day I get to lead the Hero's Day parade. I don't have time for a splinter."

So King Kenrick hopped and hobbled and limped around the royal bedroom, getting dressed for his busy day. He looked very smart and regal, but as soon as he put his shoes on, his toe began to throb.

"I know," he said. "I'll wear slippers!" He hopped over to the closet and pulled out a scarlet pair.

Although the slipper felt better than the shoe had, it still hurt his toe. He tried using only his heel to walk. But that made a funny noise. *Step, thump. Step, thump. Step, thump.*

"Goodness!" said the queen when he came into the dining room. "Why are you walking that funny way? Have you hurt your foot?"

"No!" said King Kenrick. "It's only a little splinter. Let's eat breakfast."

"A splinter!" she exclaimed. "I'll have to get it out."

"No!" said the king. "It will come out by itself."

"Nonsense! Splinters don't come out by themselves. Do they, Gloria?" the queen asked, as the cook came into the room, carrying the king's oatmeal.

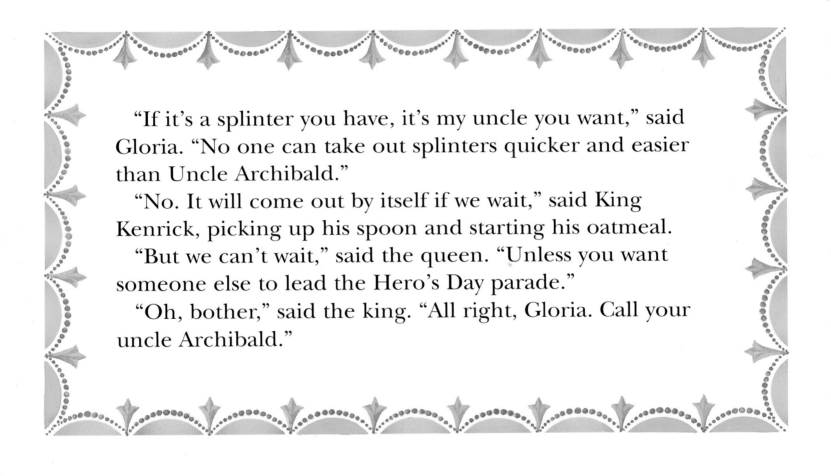

"If it's a splinter you have, it's my uncle you want," said Gloria. "No one can take out splinters quicker and easier than Uncle Archibald."

"No. It will come out by itself if we wait," said King Kenrick, picking up his spoon and starting his oatmeal.

"But we can't wait," said the queen. "Unless you want someone else to lead the Hero's Day parade."

"Oh, bother," said the king. "All right, Gloria. Call your uncle Archibald."

After breakfast the king went into the throne room to wait. He and the head footman played three games of Go Fish to help pass the time.

King Kenrick had just won the third game when Uncle Archibald's arrival was announced.

"Oh, bother," said the king. "We were just about to start a new game."

He put his slipper back on, and *step, thump, step, thump,* he followed Gloria back to his bedroom.

"Come along," the queen said to the guards. "We may be needed."

Gloria opened the bedroom door, and King Kenrick stepped in first. The room was empty! He looked at Gloria. "I thought you said your uncle was in here."

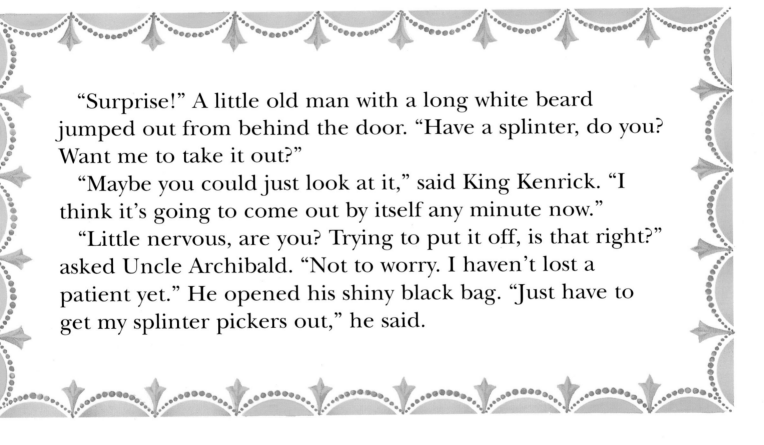

"Surprise!" A little old man with a long white beard jumped out from behind the door. "Have a splinter, do you? Want me to take it out?"

"Maybe you could just look at it," said King Kenrick. "I think it's going to come out by itself any minute now."

"Little nervous, are you? Trying to put it off, is that right?" asked Uncle Archibald. "Not to worry. I haven't lost a patient yet." He opened his shiny black bag. "Just have to get my splinter pickers out," he said.

He leaned over and pulled out a big black pair of pliers. "That's for holding the toe," he said.

Next he brought out an ice pick. "That's for finding the splinter."

Last he held up a saw. "That's in case we can't get it out and have to amputate."

"Oh, no!" wailed King Kenrick.

"Uncle, put those things away and quit teasing," Gloria said. "You're upsetting the king."

"Little joke, little joke, that's all," said Gloria's uncle, tickling his chin with the end of his beard. "Fooled you, didn't I? Well now, hop up on the bed and lie down on your stomach."

King Kenrick wasn't used to having people tell him what to do. (Except for the queen, of course.) But he climbed up on the bed and lay down.

Gloria's uncle poked at King Kenrick's toe. "Ow!" the king yelled.

"I'm just looking," Uncle Archibald said.

"Oh," said King Kenrick. "Well, be careful," he warned as he tried to pull his foot away.

"Do you need our help?" the footman asked Uncle Archibald.

"Not at all, not at all," said Uncle Archibald. "The splinter's out."

The king opened one eye. "It's what?" he asked.

"Splinter's out—it's out, I say. Got it out while you were wiggling around. Lookee here."

King Kenrick opened his other eye. Sure enough, there was the big black splinter sticking up from the tweezers. The king slid off the bed.

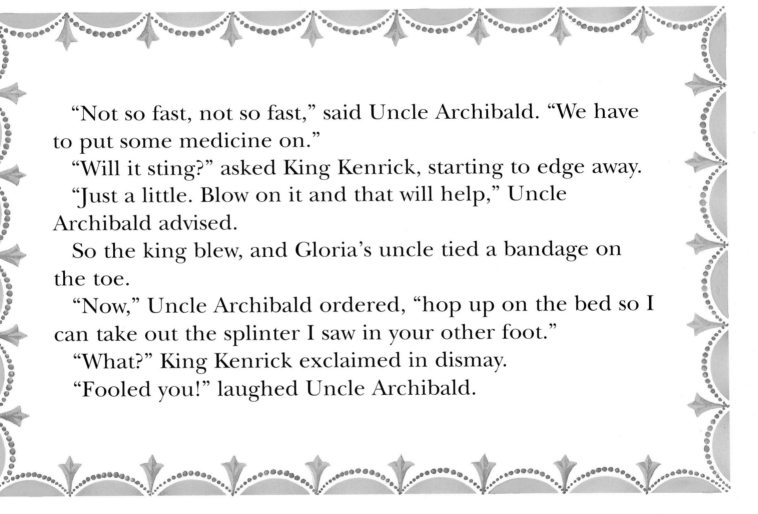

"Not so fast, not so fast," said Uncle Archibald. "We have to put some medicine on."

"Will it sting?" asked King Kenrick, starting to edge away.

"Just a little. Blow on it and that will help," Uncle Archibald advised.

So the king blew, and Gloria's uncle tied a bandage on the toe.

"Now," Uncle Archibald ordered, "hop up on the bed so I can take out the splinter I saw in your other foot."

"What?" King Kenrick exclaimed in dismay.

"Fooled you!" laughed Uncle Archibald.

"Oh, Uncle," said Gloria. "You've got to stop being such a tease!" She helped her uncle pack up his bag.

"Just a minute!" said King Kenrick. "Guards, throw that man in the dungeon!"

The guards looked surprised, but they formed a circle around Gloria's uncle.

"Lookee here!" protested Uncle Archibald, "I did you a favor, I did."

"You've been playing tricks on me all morning," said King Kenrick. "That's no way to treat the king."

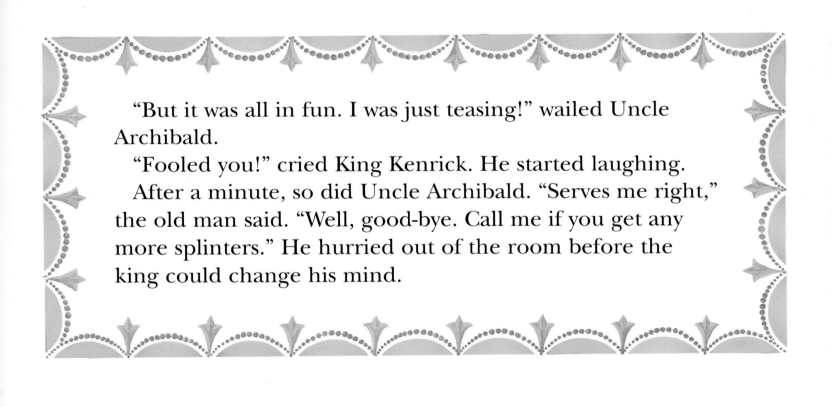

"But it was all in fun. I was just teasing!" wailed Uncle Archibald.

"Fooled you!" cried King Kenrick. He started laughing.

After a minute, so did Uncle Archibald. "Serves me right," the old man said. "Well, good-bye. Call me if you get any more splinters." He hurried out of the room before the king could change his mind.

King Kenrick marched over to the closet and pulled out his shiny black shoes. They looked much better with his uniform than the scarlet slippers had. "Now I'm ready to lead the Hero's Day parade." And he strutted out of the bedroom, feeling like a brave hero himself.